CLEAN MARGINS

AND OTHER STORIES . . .

Good
Luck —

Linda

LINDA ROCKER

Clean Margins and Other Stories . . .

Published by Wheatmark˚
1760 East River Road, Suite 145
Tucson, Arizona 85718
U.S.A.
www.wheatmark.com

ISBN: 978-1-62787-009-2
LCCN: 2013944167

For my daughter, Sara

GOSSIP

The leaves, like women interchange
  Sagacious confidence;
Somewhat of nods and somewhat of
  Portentous inference.

The parties in both cases
  Enjoining secrecy;
Inviolable compact
  To notoriety

Emily Dickinson

CONTENTS

Acknowledgments...ix

Clean Margins.. 1

Waiting... 9

The Crusader 19

Maternity...25

The Bargain 67

The Setting Sun..73

The Bride's Dance...89

Fate Is the Hunter...95

Ghost Stories 103

ACKNOWLEDGMENTS

Some of these stories are a mixture of memoir and fiction, most notably "Maternity." The remainder are fiction, albeit informed by my experiences.

I appreciate the encouragement and valuable critiques of my fellow students at workshops and conferences, but I am especially indebted to friends, relatives and editors who have turned re-reading into an art form. Thanks to Dan for his unerring eye for details, to Janice Eidus and Philip Turner for superb editing and to Kat Gautreaux for her patience.

If there is a theme to these stories, it was unintended. Nevertheless, it is apparent that they are bound by the recognition that women must address so many competing demands that it is a wonder that they can see a path to fulfillment. But, they do, and therein lies the magic I have struggled to capture.

CLEAN MARGINS

Because it is wintertime, she can see the brassy red neon sign advertising "Food" flashing on and off until midnight when the restaurant closes. The leaves don't block the view at this time of year and she's grateful for that. Looking at the sign in the distance gives her a feeling of comfort that she doesn't quite understand, but its very ordinariness quells her feelings of panic.

"We got it all," the green Nehru cap and long gown hovering over her gurney had announced. At that moment she had not cared, it had not registered. It was only later that she began to disbelieve, to feel in her gut that, like her husband's lies about his affair, the surgeon's reassurances that there was no cancer left had been merely diversions from the truth.

The cancer seemed almost banal, this one in particular. There was hardly a soft drink, clothing line or discount store that didn't feature a pink ribbon on its logo. Yet she had been surprised. There was no family history, she had assured the doctor, and she didn't deserve this additional complication in her life. He had agreed. But then, what could he have said without understanding that this might be more than she could bear at this moment.

"We're a team," he had assured her, never meeting her eye, his gaze busily measuring his work site for problems in excavation.

Her given name, Agatha, became "Aggie" before her second birthday, a fact that annoyed her mother and delighted her father who thought her name belonged to an old maid. The nickname suited her in many ways, especially in her adolescence when she epitomized the college-bound, pony tail and bangs, Shaker Heights field hockey queen. If there was something that didn't go Aggie's way, she had no memory of it. She accepted the fact that she was not beautiful, but then neither was her mother who had managed to snag a handsome, popular Ivy League graduate and who lived what Aggie thought was an absolutely perfect life.

That made everything that came later such a surprise.

She slides awkwardly in the bed, touching the bandage like an open sore, touching it for what seems the hundredth time today, as she distracts herself with the macabre trivia of her medical situation. The discharge instructions provided by the nurse had covered with clinical precision her medications, her cleansing routines, all the minutia of her "going home." But, perhaps due to oversight, the lists failed to include a remedy for reality, a cure for the new certainty that she is now deformed. And so she touches, she does not look, but she touches. It is, she thinks, not so different than her mind's masochistic need to repeatedly revisit the joint appointment with her husband's psychiatrist shortly before her surgery.

"This is not all that unusual given these circumstances," said the squat, expressionless man as he slid open his desk drawer to sneak a look at his notes. "Many men feel helpless in the face of a wife's cancer—especially, of course, a cancer that may be life threatening. You shouldn't take it personally."

She moves her hand away from the incision and lays it on her belly. The medication must be wearing off and she debates the risk of taking the next dose before it is time. She turns cautiously onto her "good" side, surveying the room with momentary pleasure. The best part of the room, the part she adores, is the wall opposite the bed. It is entirely filled, from floor to ceiling, with books. The upper shelves house her collections from graduate school: Coleridge, Keats, Shelley and an incomplete set of Eliot that seems to announce its deficiency by sliding down on the shelf.

It is apparent that the organizers of these shelves had a plan. The books are arranged by size in some instances (best sellers and paperbacks), by literary value in others and, in the case of "topics of special interest," by the need for filler or ballast.

It was in part their love of literature that had brought them together in the first place. They were both married, but not to each other. At parties they had drifted together, talking with a large group that grew smaller and smaller as their talk became more esoteric and their intense focus on one another became more obvious. It did not feel intentional, this stroll along the edge of a precipice. And yet, the moment came when they leapt with abandon, mindless of the cost to others, mindful only of themselves and their passion.

A pair of divorces and a marriage later, they had filled these bookshelves, carefully creating an opening, a "shrine-like" space, for the glass sculpture they had received as a wedding gift. Etched across the middle of the clear glass heart had been the words "Good Morning. I love you." But like the design for their marriage, the sculpture has disappeared, and now a small television has intruded into the space, its unwelcome occupation testified to by the black cords that run offensively down the front of the bookshelf and across the floor to an outlet The shards of glass that had flown everywhere in the geyser of her rage when she discovered his betrayal might still cling to the top of the bookshelves, hidden from view, but they are clear and sparkling in her memory.

"Did you think he began this affair only after my diagnosis?" she had inquired of her husband's shrink, who had the unlikely and ill-fitting nickname, Duke. "He's been involved with her for a very long time and surely you know that she is not the first." She pauses to catch her breath. "In fact, you probably think that I'm the one who needs a therapist since I've put up with this for so many years." His silence was meant to say nothing, but says everything—everything he knows about her, about her husband, about them. It was way too much information for anyone to have secondhand.

"Shit," she says, brought back from the sinkhole of her memories as she looks down at the widening damp circle on her T-shirt. It's time to drain the tubes. She's already regretting her decision to send the visiting nurse home with false assurances that others will be coming to help her. Then again, she really can't stand the woman's incessant babbling.

She pulls her body up and swings her legs to the side of the bed. As always, the width and depth of the pain surprise her. It rolls around the incision and spreads like molten lava down her body and out onto the bedclothes, pooling and congealing while her breathing slows to accommodate its rhythm.

She reaches for the chair, a perfect bedroom chair, covered in soft and forgiving muslin, patterned with pale blue flowers. It was never intended to serve as anything other than a way station for a robe, but her father sits in it during his daily visits. He moves it around to better see the small television and they watch together, talking occasionally about politics, news and her grown children.

When he leaves, he puts the chair back in its place and carefully folds her robe (which was thrown there haphazardly before he arrived) and places it on the seat. He doesn't mean to embarrass her by this, but she is relieved by his departure. Though she is touched that he wants to do something, anything that will help, his very powerlessness frightens her

As she steps into the slick granite bathroom, she wonders if her husband has removed his clothes from their closet. "It's all got to go, out of my sight," she had pleaded. He had walked out of her hospital room before she could finish the sentence, seal the indictment. She now sees, as she turns the corner, that he has not done as she had asked. A stab of rage hits her and she grabs the sink edge to prevent acting on her impulse to pull down everything of his and hurl it out the window.

She looks again at the closet, at the high rods for him, the low ones for her. She will notice the absence of his clothes. She will know the absence of his smell. She will need to reclaim this space-reclaim it like all the other spaces in her life. Excising his wardrobe will be the easy part.

"You win," he had said, unwilling to explore the nooks and crannies of their broken history, instead making it yet another competition. Friends assured her that he was in "lust," not love. But the borders of their pairing had been breached and, like her mother before her, she preferred her rage to rapprochement. "Listen, Ag," her father pleaded, "you shouldn't use your mother and me as role models in this situation. Everyone is different."

Fussing with the drains that disgust, but also excite her with the possibility that they carry away lingering bits of disease, she thinks that she is not so unique. Great writers will not immortalize the duality of betrayals she has suffered. No ballad will harmonize the cancer that found her body's weakness with the woman who found her husband's.

Aggie turns away from the large mirror, sparing herself further reflection of any kind. She will return to her bed, to her medication that will color all the blues and whites and everything around her a different hue—a muddied purple that will soften the edges of her anger and walk her easily into oblivion.

"Wake up, Aggie." The words blast through the codeine haze and disappear into the vast space of her dreams. She does not want to open her eyes because no one will be there, and she will be awake, alone and with hours of fear and pain until she can swallow the magic pill again.

She looks up to see him towering over her.

"Please, just leave," she mutters turning her head away from him. But she knows he won't. He's itching for a fight. There are not enough fights in the world for him.

Her eyes have closed again, but she hears him in the bathroom slamming drawers, muttering to himself. She dozes, feeling a strange contentment that she is in a place he cannot inhabit.

"I'm going to leave my set of keys at the gatehouse so you won't need to worry about my coming again unannounced." He hoists his bulging white plastic garbage bag and leaves the room.

"Wait!" she shouts. "Wait, please!" She hears the plastic bag hit the floor. His face, so achingly familiar, appears in the doorway. He waits.

She has waited, also. She gets out of the bed knowing how gaunt and disheveled she looks. She moves slowly toward him and hands him a package wrapped in newspaper and twine.

"Here" she says, drinking in the expectant look on his face. "Here are the flannel sheets you and your girlfriend fucked on while I was in the hospital."

For a minute she thinks he will cry, his face flushed with the heat of her anger.

She celebrates her revenge as she hears the front door close. She has cut deeply. But these margins will not be clean.

WAITING

"Harry, close the damn door!"

Myra's eyes opened slowly, just long enough for the sliver of light from the bathroom to cut like a scalpel into her brain. She raised herself up on her elbows and stared hard at the bathroom, hoping that her frustration would free float into Harry's consciousness. It was no use. Harry would emerge when he was good and ready.

She tried to get comfortable, but she felt constricted by the narrow twin size bed, a recent replacement for the large, ambitious king-size affair that had dominated this bedroom for nearly fifty years. In daylight, she could still see the depressions of the former bed's footprint in the plush mauve carpeting. Its headboard, a towering wall of faux leather studded along the borders with brass nails, had announced that this was an important place. Likewise, the layers of satiny sheets and overstuffed duvets covered in garden prints, each perfectly coordinated with the carpet and curtains, had left no doubt that these people were, if not royalty, certainly occupants of means.

The move to twin beds had been a relief for both her and Harry, each of them wanting just a little more space and privacy for their nocturnal flatulence, for Harry's sleep apnea that required a mask and a machine loud as a jackhammer, and for their discordant duet of snores. The decorator had assured her that the mahogany-whorled headboards would be handsome and would coordinate with the remains of the color scheme and style, but she still felt as though she and Harry had been invaded by the old people squads, people who think anything will do because after a certain age, taste and standards are not only unnecessary, they're impermissible luxuries.

And perhaps they were right. If she allowed her mind to slide over to the memory side, that side of her brain where she had stored all the important moments, the pictures, the faces, the dialogue that still aroused such deep feelings that they sometimes frightened and confused her, she would have to think about that king size bed and about the sex. It had been so important once, doing it right, doing it more than once, doing it with the moans and groans made by the girls in those films they rented when Harry got nervous about himself, doing it with a little blue pill that required an appointment. Myra never quite understood what all the moaning and groaning was about. But when Harry took his time, when he put his hand down there and moved it around in a soft, tender way, she got feelings of real pleasure and that was enough for her.

Myra flopped back on the bed, resigned to waiting. She turned on her side so she wouldn't see him when he came out of the bathroom. He refused to wear pajamas, not even a t-shirt or boxers. "I've slept naked every night of my life since I got out of the fucking army. When I was on Iwo Jima, my ass didn't feel fresh air for a month. Fucking stunk so bad I could hardly bend over and breathe at the same time."

When they were young, Myra had found his nakedness daring and sexy. Now she dreaded looking at him. His testicles, that once looked like their nickname—round and bouncy—hung loosely like shriveled sacks of old onions. And his wonderful rear end, smooth and tight with a small mole near the top of the crack that resembled a beauty mark on a glamour girl's cheek—that gorgeous butt now drooped long and low. And the beauty mark? Well, it had a few hairs growing from the middle of it.

She, on the other hand, had possessed precious little in body baggage to sag as she aged, Unlike her friends with enviable cleavage in their youth, whatever of her bust fell, it was welcome as it gave a hint of the breasts she had always wished for and never had-not even during her two pregnancies. She had been a skinny kid and now she was a withered older woman, her underarms dancing around like dress flounces as she walked. She had once taken great pride in her taut body, but now when she caught an unplanned glimpse of herself in the hall mirror, she knew that her grandmother's generation was right—a little schmaltz around the middle and you didn't suffer the march of lines around your mouth and cheeks.

Nothing about her appearance, or his for that matter, meant very much these days. Harry told her every morning that she was as beautiful as the day they met and since everything in their lives was now a ritual—what they said, what they ate, when they went out and what they wore—this compliment from Harry was always followed by his departure from the breakfast table with a comment about going to see a man about a dog.

Myra realized as she pulled the crisply ironed sheet toward her shoulders that the room was unpleasantly warm. It was a reminder that she needed to call the handyman. She had a list of issues that needed attention and Harry loved to tease her that the only thing that didn't appear on her list was a note reminding her to look at the goddamn list. Well, the whacky thermostat would be reminder enough, especially if her grown children came by to check on them. The first thing they'd say after hello was, "O my God, how can you stand it in here? It's like a furnace." She smiled in the almost dark room, thinking that it was only fair, since whenever she went to their homes to visit she brought her winter coat to shelter her from the blast of their air conditioning.

There was no sound from the bathroom. She would have to give up soon, drag herself out of bed, stomp over, close the door, and try to find sleep, knowing that the whole process would begin again when he came out, climbed in bed and muttered to her before he dove into his mask, "Honey, the light's on in the bathroom. Turn it out, please. I can't sleep with all that brightness." She'd want to bolt out of her bed, pounce on him with her fists flying and reduce him to pleas for mercy. Instead, she would sigh deeply and loudly (a waste of effort since the machine noise drowned out whatever was left of his hearing) and walk across the room to close the door with an elaborately martyred gesture.

But to do otherwise, to sit down with Harry for a serious conversation about the light, his indifference to her needs, or anything else for that matter, would be a waste of time and effort. They laughed about being "old dogs" and about their resistance to any kind of change, but the truth was far more serious and depressing. It simply didn't matter. Neither of them any longer cared if the saucer matched the coffee cup or if the spill in the refrigerator had begun to change color before it was finally wiped. Likewise, the appearance of unmatched socks or dissonant plaids and stripes was more frequently than not disregarded, whereas a decade earlier they would have caused a sartorial tirade.

Myra wondered briefly if there was any conversation that plumbed the surface of their indifferent lives. The most shocking thing about these mundane exchanges with Harry was that neither of them seemed to mind the loss—the disappearance of their snappy patter, dazzling wit and profoundly thoughtful conversation that had been a cornerstone of their relationship for so many years. It had seemed effortless back then, but it would be exhausting today. "It must be me," she thought. Her conversations with their daughter were equally superficial and sometimes downright disingenuous.

"How are you feeling, Mom?" their daughter would ask, the background noise of her computer clearly audible. Myra's replies were perfectly scripted to sound upbeat and uncomplaining. They would exchange news like strangers on a bus, avoiding any hint of discontent or disagreement. But neither of them was fooled, both of them sensing the rip tides nagging at their ankles ready to drag them into deeper water without warning.

By contrast, her son took her every word at face value, an attitude that struck her as uncaring, but that made Harry far happier. Neither child was foolish enough to press for the truth, for a candid edition of their parents' most recent challenges or frustrations. Myra was sympathetic about their avoidance, for she knew only too well the price to be paid for insisting on full disclosure. The bliss of ignorance had rescued her on more than one occasion in her marriage from asking Harry questions, dumb questions, about whether he still loved her or found her sexually attractive. To know more than she knew already made both of them responsible.

The sound of glass breaking brought Myra bolt upright. She was already out of her bed when she heard the thud. Harry was on the floor between the sink and the built-in bathtub. Myra grabbed Harry's hand, reached for a towel to staunch the flow of blood spreading from the back of his head and yelled, "Don't do this, Harry! God Damn It! Don't do this." She realized that she was screaming and clamped her hand hard across her mouth, waiting for her breathing to slow and now feeling the wetness of her tears fill the hollow of her palm. She knew that she needed to call someone—isn't that why the emergency phone numbers were plastered all over the house, on telephones and bulletin boards and the refrigerator door? But she was afraid to leave him here alone. "Oh, Harry," she said softly, as she leaned back against the cold tile of the bathtub.

When the rescue squad arrived, they found the front door open wide. Myra was seated on the colonial wing chair that had always been her favorite, but which she knew instinctively she would forever associate with the pain of this night. "Was this the first heart attack, Ma'am?" The young man in a slightly oversized uniform was in front of her on one knee, like a suitor making a marriage proposal. Myra shook her head, both in answer to the question and in an effort to shake the kaleidoscope pieces back into some recognizable order, as she remembered the cardiologist's reassurances after the by-pass surgery a few years earlier.

"You're a new man, Harry. If you play by the rules, two things will happen: Your short game will improve and you'll live a lot longer." Harry had nodded in apparent acquiescence, but Myra knew better. Harry would not give up the things he loved; the fatty foods, the Dewar's White Label, the easy chair that he joked gave him cardiac exercise every time it threatened to tip over when he flopped into it. "It's my Goddamn life,

15

Myra, and I'd rather have less of it than live it in misery." Myra didn't argue with him, not so much because she didn't know what was coming, but because she saw his point.

Now, as she stood in the receiving line outside the sanctuary, she marveled at how quickly the magnitude of her loss had appeared and impressed itself on her. She desperately wished she could tell Harry about the cousin who still owed Harry money showing up in a Bentley with his new wife, a real looker, on his pinstriped arm. And who could she laugh with about their friend, Sol, appearing without his toupee, as though his rug would somehow tarnish the sincerity of his grief? In fact, as the line moved at an agonizingly slow pace, she had mentally catalogued each person's place in their history as a married couple, discovering later that she could remember almost nothing of who had attended, what had been said or how she had felt at the time.

After the funeral and after the company and the food were finished and gone, Myra sat at the breakfast table and stared out the window. She knew in some distant way, like a radio playing in another room too soft to understand the words, but loud enough to know it was music, that there were things to be done. She should start a new list, but she didn't have the energy to get a pencil and paper, let alone force her mind to focus on all the details that needed her attention. Even the offers of help from friends and her children did nothing to motivate her to organize the mounting evidence of everything that Harry had taken care of for them and that she knew next to nothing about. It embarrassed her and if he had been there they would have had one of their arguments about who does what for whom in the relationship. No one ever prevailed, but you'd have thought there was big money on the outcome to listen to the two of them going at it.

Looking around the kitchen, Myra could see that the help had done a good job of cleaning up after the mourners. She left the table and went to the kitchen sink. She turned on the water for no reason and let it run. She stood there like a statue and waited for Harry to shout from the living room, "Turn off the water, Myra. You're gonna bankrupt us for Chris-sakes." She stood listening to the rush of wet sound for what seemed like hours, remembering how mad she'd be at those moments. Mad that he didn't understand that her hands were deep in a mound of ground chuck and eggs while she tried to form a ball that would, with luck, become a meatloaf. Mad that someone always seemed to be looking over her shoulder with a suggestion or a criticism. *Oh, dear God, if I could just be alone,* she'd say to herself, picturing a time when nobody would have dominion over her.

She felt guilty now that such thoughts of her widowhood had ever seemed appealing. She wished desperately that they could have just one more of their late afternoon cocktail hours when they would sit together, sip their drinks and talk to each other. She would tell him that although she had been crazy about him, she hadn't always loved him. She would apologize for blaming him for things that he couldn't fix or for things he didn't even understand. She would ask him to please wait for her, wher-ever he was now, to please wait because nobody was left in the world who knew as much about her or understood her better.

It was close to her bedtime and this would be her first night without any relative or friend staying with her. She carefully followed her night-time routine and climbed into her bed. She inhaled the quiet, not missing the racket made by Harry's machine. She arranged the sheets, plumped her pillow, let her eyelids slide toward her cheeks and after what seemed like hours of sleeplessness, she sighed loudly, got out of bed and opened the bathroom door to let in a sliver of light.

THE
CRUSADER

The door to the toilet stall swung out and nearly knocked me flat on my keister. I caught my balance as the heavyset woman pushed by me. She said nothing to me, not "excuse me" or anything like that. I started to walk into the flat, plastic wall cubicle that still smelled of her baby powder perfume when I made a snap decision. "Hey lady," I said in my very most polite and quiet voice, "why don't you come back here and clean up your mess?"

She was a big woman and when she turned away from the sink, I could see she was old. Not ancient, but old enough to know better. Her gray-streaked hair was thinning and showed some scalp in the front. She had deep lines on her forehead that were double-creased because of her frown.

"I beg your pardon?" she said to me. "Are you speaking to me?" She was staring at me wide-eyed and I could see she was getting a little red in the face.

"You know I'm talking to you, Ma'am," I said in my most modulated voice. "Frankly, I'm getting a little tired of people like you who don't care about anybody but themselves. They just go about their self-serving little business, leave their messes for other people to clean up and think nothing of it." I noticed that there were now some other women around us and they were giving each other looks. You know, the kind of looks that say: "Hey we've got us a situation here. Is there gonna be trouble?" I'd seen those looks before and heard the whispered words that always came after: crazy, weird, looney. *Always judging*, I thought to myself, *these people looked you over, gave you a low grade for being different, for sticking up for your values, and dumped you like yesterday's cat litter.*

The balding woman was looking really agitated. I hated that. People should be able to manage stressful encounters with a kind of matter-of-fact style, like I did.

"Listen," I wanted to say, "I've spent my life trying to make the world a better place. I marched for animal rights and for lettuce and I've signed a lot of petitions, a lot." It wasn't really true, of course. But I thought about it a lot, all the crusades we heard about back when I was at parochial school, like the nuns thought it was our job to out-Jesus Jesus.

Well, this was my mission today and I was determined to teach a lesson to anyone who left her pee on the toilet seat for the next person to sit down on, especially at a classy bookstore. So, instead of lecturing this lady on her sacrilegious and selfish behavior, I made a sweeping bow and gestured toward the door from which she had emerged. I admit it was theatrical, but then from the looks I was getting from the rest of my audience, this was pretty high drama anyway.

And speaking of looks, let me assure you this was no ordinary, Greyhound bus stop bathroom. Not by a long shot. The counters were marble with waves of gray and pink and the soap dispensers looked like pretty little seashells and gave out foamy stuff to wash your hands with. I liked this bathroom and I came to this bookstore almost every day on my morning break from the fancy grocery store at the other end of the mall—that is if you can call ten minutes away from arranging cans of snap peas on a shelf a real break.

Most men I know (which is basically my father and brothers) have no idea about women's bathrooms. To them a john is a john. Ask any guy what kind of marble is on the counter in his dumper and he'll go totally blank. But check with a woman about where she needs to go to do her business and she can name chapter and verse on every toilet in town. So it's not like this woman's transgression was minor. It affected more than half the registered voters in America, for God's sake!

The people standing around staring at us had slowly backed out of the bathroom and now it was just the two of us again. It was a "high noon" situation if ever there was one and this woman was obviously not going to cooperate.

"Look," I said "I know you think I'm nuts, but this has been kind of eating away at me for a long time. We're talking thousands, maybe millions of victims—women with damp panties who have to walk around the rest of the day like that."

She was wearing oversized black pants with an elastic waist. She wasn't sloppy or anything like that, but she didn't have a neat (my mother used to say "finished") look about her. She wasn't wearing much make-up on and the only jewelry on her was a narrow gold watch with an old fashioned oval face. Because she was overweight, the skin on her wrists made a little cushion on each side of the watchband.

"Can I just leave?' the woman asked in this little voice that really kind of got on my nerves. "I didn't mean to offend you," she whined, "but I'd just like to be on my way."

Well, that really did it! It might have been better if she hadn't said anything at all, but it was too late for that. I walked over to the foamy stuff, maybe stomped over, because as usual I was going to have to do the job myself, and before I knew what was happening she was yelling, "Help me, help me somebody! She's going to kill me." And with that she ran out the door.

I calmly walked out right after her and saw that a crowd of people had gathered around the doorway. I looked at their faces, all screwed up with fear and I could feel it. It was kind of disgusting to me that they didn't get it. Not the guys, ya know, cause for them it's not such a problem. But the women—well, it pushed me right over the proverbial edge.

"Fuck you all!" I screamed turning in a half-circle, "There oughta be a law against broads like her hovering like a drone over the damn toilet seat and leaving it all sprinkled like somebody's front lawn. What happened to manners, for Chrissake?"

I'd spoken my piece and I would have waited around for someone to get up the nerve to thank me for saying exactly what they'd been thinking in bathrooms all over town, but even I wasn't crazy enough to do that. I've had some close calls before—no mob scenes, mind you—but some kind of worked up people who didn't like the younger generation taking the time to point out their failings. This crowd looked just as unappreciative.

It was like Moses parting the Red Sea. I took one step and the group just made a path for me to stroll through.

"I'm telling you this story, Doctor, because I'm proud of myself. I see it as a story of courage and, brother, let me tell you that these places should be called anything but *restrooms*. It can get intense in these confined spaces, really intense."

I paused and drew a deep breath. The man sitting across from me behind the desk was looking down at God knows what while he scribbled notes. His glasses were crooked and his hair looked like the edges on a sofa pillow. The office was brown. I don't mean taupe or beige or any of those fancy places on the far end of the color strip. I mean brown and ugly. The more I thought about it the more I noticed how shabby he looked, with his rumpled jacket and hairy ears. Some people might have said something, like "Hey there, Doc, I don't mean to be judging here, but this place looks like crap and you're not far behind."

But I always try to be fair and not judgmental. If you're going to fix the world, you need to be tolerant. My favorite nun in school, Sister Mary Margaret, told us in no uncertain terms about how to be a warrior for Christ. "Tell them the truth, teach them obedience and celebrate the good you do for others." *Damn, but that fit me to "T."*

"It's a pretty inspiring story, don't you think, Doc? I like a story with a moral." I said. "Truth is, I don't know why I'm telling you about it except I guess you're getting paid to listen. Right, Doc?"

"Right."

MATERNITY

November 8, 2012
Cleveland
Linda

This morning:

Nice girls are not supposed to despise their Grandmas. So maybe I'm not a nice girl, but if you read this story, most of which I know to be true, you will understand why I hate the woman who caused my mother, Harriet, such unimaginable pain.

I know only one version of my mother's life and experiences, up to and including my adult years with her. I don't know anyone still living who can correct what my brothers and I learned in bits and pieces during the course of her life. But, if there is slander in the telling, the blame lies squarely at the feet of those who could have told the truth when they had the chance and chose otherwise

I've taken liberties with scenes that I heard about or presume occurred. But the essence of the harm done to an innocent child is indisputable and its exposure is long overdue.

December 24, 1915
Cleveland
Jen

The limp always gave her trouble, especially in cold weather. She had developed a loping gait to compensate for the swaying and tilting of her body, but walking on the uneven cobbled streets around the Cleveland steelyards was still difficult and hazardous. Despite the danger, the trip to the mill every day was worth it to Jeanette Leavitt. She knew she was lucky to have this job, a real job that paid a decent salary. The position of bookkeeper set Jen apart from all the women who worked for meager wages as secretaries or clerks. When Jen had attended night school in downtown Cleveland, she was the only woman in the class, a fact that impressed many of her family and neighbors. Although it was a source of great pride for her, she was acutely aware that in the pre-war community of Cleveland Jews, many of them immigrants or first generation offspring, the only "degree" that mattered was the one a woman obtained standing under the *chupa*, the ritual wedding canopy. Nearing the age of thirty, she would soon be considered a spinster, an uncommon fate in an era when arranged marriages were still tolerated by women and when almost any female capable of reproduction was wed—the younger the better.

"Say Miss Jeanette, are you going to favor us with your beautiful presence at the holiday party this afternoon?" Harry Sherman was the owner's son and he evidently felt it was part of his job description to flirt with every woman at the plant. The fact that he was quite handsome had always seemed to provide him a passport to many rumored dalliances with secretaries, as well as most of the cooks from the company cafeteria.

Jen did not bother to look up from her account books. She was aware from the comments made by friends of the family that she was very attractive, tall with a peaches and cream complexion and eyes of cerulean blue. But experience, including the frank appraisals of her brothers, had convinced her that her limp, coupled with her acerbic tongue, made her a less than desirable woman for the average guy. "But, don't worry Sis," her brothers would console her, "there's a guy for every gal. You'll meet someone swell who'll fall like a ton of bricks for those baby blues." She regarded their appraisal of her chances for matrimony as worthless cheerleading. Her limp was a telling vestige of childhood polio and although the family had fabricated stories about her fall from a horse, no one who heard them was fooled and no one wanted a cripple for a wife or a daughter-in-law.

Jen had no intention of hanging around for the holiday party. Her parents were religious Jews and although Jen disdained their adherence to the innumerable rules and practices required of them by their ortho-doxy, she nonetheless considered herself a Jew by birth. She would leave the celebrations to Harry Sherman and his co-workers. She felt his pres-ence hovering over her desk and when she didn't answer him, she as-sumed he'd walked away and had decided to leave her alone.

It was apparent that the party was already underway, as the large room in which she worked processing orders was now empty. It was only mid-afternoon, but the light was already growing dim, made murkier by the dust and smoke from the mills. Jen moved slowly toward the hooks where her coat and scarf hung and reached for the stick she used to lend her balance on the icy streets.

The strong arms suddenly reaching around Jen's mid-section made her gasp loudly. "I refuse to go to this party alone. I insist that you let me put a smile where that scowl has taken up permanent residence." Pulling away from Harry's unwelcome embrace, she lost her balance and found herself caught in his arms again, but this time facing him. Jen was speechless for the first time in her life. Harry took her stunned look as consent, pulling her along through the Billing Department door and toward the cafeteria, never pausing as she struggled to keep up with him.

The cafeteria was festooned with colorful balloons hanging randomly from the wooden rafters. Miniature Christmas trees were scattered indifferently on the long picnic tables that ran from one side of the room to the other and the plates of chips and nuts had already spilled their salty contents on the benches and floor. Harry guided Jen toward the bar at the far end of the rectangular room, a makeshift affair of slatted boxes atop which were wobbling bottles of whiskey and a cheap imitation champagne having only bubbles in common with the real thing. The sounds of lively conversation and the accordion were intoxicating without anything more and suddenly Jen became greedy with her desire to really be in this moment. In one long gulp she drank the bubbly that Harry handed to her. He seemed delighted with the change in her mood and demeanor. Although no amount of alcohol could disconnect her from the ever-present shame of her limp, nor allow her to dance in public, she found herself swaying with the music, her arm linked in Harry's, close to his chest and stiff collar that smelled vaguely of men's shaving tonic mixed with sweat.

It was nearly midnight when the couple approached the small, frame house on Orange Avenue. Jen's father was seated on the porch swing and she realized with a start that he had been waiting for her for hours in the bitter cold. Without looking back at Harry, she climbed the stairs and disappeared into the house.

Harry, who had not moved from his spot on the sidewalk, tipped his fedora toward Fishel Leavitt before he turned and walked rapidly toward the streetcar stop.

No one in the house said anything to Jen about the incident. In fact, it would be nearly six months before any reference was made to that night or to Harry Sherman. But by then it was too late.

September 9, 1916
Chicago
Jen

"It helps to scream. Go ahead, if you like, Mrs. Sherman. We're all alone here." But she would not scream. She would not embarrass herself further. The humiliation of this endless day was bad enough—a punishment she knew she deserved. There was not enough pain in the world to satisfy her self-loathing.

"Go ahead, Jeanette. It will be all right. You'll see. You won't remember a thing."

Jen turned her eyes toward the woman in her starched white apron and pointed cap standing beside her bed. "You are a stupid young girl," Jen almost spat at the nurse,"it will never be alright." There was a brief pause. And then she screamed.

The birth certificate for the baby girl born a few hours later stated the mother was a housewife. It listed her name as Jeanette Harris. It said she was married to a salesman named Harry Sherman of Lynchburg, West Virginia. It gave the child's name as Harriet. Among these declarations, only the name of the child was not a lie.

Records of live births in 1916 were not kept as thoroughly as they are today, often omitting information regarding the identity of the parents or the proof of marriage. The nurses at Michael Reese Hospital were surely curious about the mother who during her "laying-in period" had no visitors and no appearance by the baby's father. During the day she barely spoke, but at night she could be heard weeping softly and humming foreign lullabies to no one. The baby girl, Harriet, would not hear these songs, at least not from Jeanette, since the nurses were given strict instructions that the newborn was never to be seen by her birth mother. After all, no one in the family wanted this child, no one came forward to claim her and in no time at all she would be the property of the Chicago Home for Orphans. Once the baby's banishment was generally known among the staff, they avoided Jen, not wanting to see the face of a woman who could abandon her own flesh and blood. And Jen? She also could not bear it and had the nurses remove the small, round mirror above the dresser.

June 16, 1922
Youngstown, Ohio
Jen and Harriet

In the summer of 1922, Youngstown, Ohio, was a veritable boomtown. Everything was going right for this small city on the edge of a vibrant tri-state area. The population had exploded in recent years and the nearby river and railroads meant a steady stream of commerce for steel plants, lumberyards and all kinds of manufacturing in Pennsylvania, West Virginia, and Ohio.

It was also a perfect place to bring a family with a secret.

Fishel Leavitt's new house on Warren Street was a sprawling wooden structure with a large porch curving around the front and sides. The green metal outdoor furniture was not welcoming to a six-year old, yet Harriet loved to sit on it and watch the sleek looking automobiles honk and sputter past the house. Her brothers talked constantly about what a great business the selling of automobiles would become, pressing Fishel to consider investing in a dealership. But her "father," nearly sixty years old now, wanted nothing to do with a new venture. He'd already closed a marginally profitable kosher meat business in Cleveland to move the family to Youngstown.

The move had been costly for everyone. Fishel's wife, Leah, was deeply resentful of being uprooted from her neighborhood in Cleveland in order to hide in this small town and care for an unwanted, illegitimate grandchild. "Yes, yes!" she had all but screamed at her husband when Jen's pregnancy became too obvious to ignore. "We'll have to send her away. But she should stay away. Have the child, give it up and stay away. You can't keep these things a secret. Someone will find out and then it's shame on us all."

Fishel had simply stared at this small, mean-spirited woman who had been chosen for him in the old country—a "devil's choice," since at the time he'd needed a wife to help him run his new lumber business in the small Polish border town where he'd grown up. It hadn't seemed to matter very much then. Young and optimistic, he believed the synagogue elders who assured him that such planned marriages always worked out—especially for the man. "What a package!" they'd chortled, "In one small step, you acquire a worker for a lifetime, a housekeeper, a bed-mate and a cook. All this for a few kopeks and a horse. Hah, lucky man!"

But Fishel Leavitt felt that the joke had been on him, even after they came to America and he was intoxicated with the promise of freedom and success, even after the births of their six children who gave him such pleasure, especially the four boys. His sense of regret was for himself and for Leah, both of them deprived of that most essential of human pleasures, love. Still, in it's absence, they had become warily compatible, moving cautiously out of the way of each other's sore spots, whether in public or private times. Until Jen's pregnancy, it had seemed to work. But as he looked now at his wife's face, red with rage, he knew it would never work again.

"You are correct, Leah, that she will leave here and have the child in another place. But then she and the child will come home and we will care for them as best we can. We will move ourselves, if we must. But we will not abandon our blood." Leah's mottled and tear-stained face was obscured, covered by balled fists still clutching at her apron. She said nothing more about it that day or for all the succeeding days while Jen spent the remainder of her pregnancy with cousins in Chicago who, when absolutely necessary, introduced her as a distant relative whose husband had been drafted in January to serve America in the Great War and who, God only knew, might never return.

It was only after news of the birth reached them that Leah confronted her husband. "If Jen must come home, then she must and I will bear it. But she will come alone. I will not have a whore *and* a bastard under my roof at the same time." Leah left the house before he could respond, which was just as well. He had never struck his wife, never considered violence against her (or anyone for that matter) until this moment. He was relieved that she had left the house—but his relief was short-lived, for she soon reappeared with their rabbi in tow.

Leah knew Fishel very well, so well that she never doubted the weight that the opinion of the rabbi would carry with her husband. Hours passed while Leah and her other daughter Rose stood in the kitchen listening to the argument that raged in the front room. Every now and then there was a pause, as if the combatants were exhausted or, perhaps, finished with their debate. But then it would begin again, the voices growing louder, the smacking of the table or the squeak of the rocking chair more pronounced, and the shouts of indignation more audible and frequent.

Finally, when it was time for the rabbi to race back for the evening prayers, Fishel accompanied him to the sidewalk, came into the house and made straight for his study. No one saw him or heard him for the rest of that night or into the next day until the sound of the wooden screen door slamming told them that he had left for the early mourners' service at the synagogue. Although he attended the morning prayer group daily, it was for his grandchild, forever lost to him, for whom he prayed on this day. And it was for his soul, and for his wife's, that he begged forgiveness from God. He had been weak, and against every instinct and belief he held dear, he had agreed to discard the flesh of his flesh as if she were a feral cat. As he looked up at the rabbi leading the service, he was filled with loathing for himself and for this spiritual leader who had led them astray at their time of greatest need. He felt trapped.

Jen returned home to the house in Cleveland within a week of her daughter's birth, while the baby was placed in an orphanage for adoption. The location and name of the agency was kept a secret from everyone, including Jen.

Leah was silent and spoke to Jen only when absolutely necessary. Fishel greeted his older daughter with a look of such profound sadness that she was unable to hold his gaze. Jen soon found herself avoiding everyone except her younger sister Rose. The two sisters had fought constantly as children, vying for time in front of the bathroom mirror, angling for use of the sewing machine in the alcove off their parents' bedroom. Rose, however, was now a married woman living in her own home. Even so, she stopped by the house almost every day on her way to or from work to console and comfort Jen. Her support, however, was as lame as her ambivalence was obvious. She could not help but disapprove of her older sister's behavior and the pain it had caused her mother and, especially, her father.

Jen was increasingly isolated. She refused to see anyone outside of her immediate family. In fact, she spent most of her time in the third floor room she had earlier shared with Rose. If she was also mourning the loss of her child, she shared those feelings with no one. What could be seen and felt by everyone, however, was that her limp seemed more pronounced than ever and her sharp tongue now cut deeper, as though to inflict pain on others equal to her own.

But that would be impossible. Whatever the degree or depth of Jen's misery, it was less excruciating than the agony suffered by Fishel Leavitt. He was a deeply religious man, a man who honored the traditions, studied the scholars and prophets and, joyfully, announced to anyone who would listen to it, the story of his personal relationship with God. And so, on the morning after the first snowfall of the year, without any notice to Leah or Jen, Fishel Leavitt left his home at dawn and returned long after dark with a three-month old baby girl in his arms. Leah, who had been asleep for hours, felt a tap on her cheek.

"Get up, wife, and feed your new daughter." Fishel placed the baby on the bed, drew Leah's arm across Harriet's tiny body, and went into his study, firmly closing the solid wood door behind him. It had been a miserable and long train ride to Chicago and he had literally wept when the headmistress of the orphanage on Clark Street had brought him the small bundle with an oversized name tag that announced "Harriet, girl, available." He would be eternally grateful for the gentle sway of the single-rail Interurban that carried him and the sleeping child home. It had not occurred to him to ask anyone what he should do if she'd awakened. The bottle and diapers supplied to him by the orphanage would have needed the help of a stranger, preferably female. Men of Fishel's generation had almost no physical contact with babies and he was not an exception to that rule. Still, the small bundle he held in his arms for six hours became a part of him and a bond was formed that remained strong for the rest of his life.

It would take him nearly a month to sell the meat market in Cleveland and find a suitable home in Youngstown. When he moved his family into their new home in the smaller city, he made it his business to take the imposing large, black pram with the small, blonde baby girl around the block, introducing his daughter, Harriet, to the neighbors. If anyone thought it strange that a man of Fishel's age had fathered a child so late in life, they kept it to themselves. Perhaps the mother was a new wife who wanted a family of her own. By the time they met Leah Leavitt, a woman far too old to conceive a child of her own, they were puzzled, then perplexed, then almost critical and finally bored. If Fishel's strolls through the neighborhood helped to staunch the inevitable gossip and speculation about the baby in their midst, Leah's near invisibility removed the only reminder that the child's parentage was, at best, suspect.

It was not a happy household, although the presence of an attractive, winsome youngster like Harriet should have lightened the mood. But Leah's bitterness at receiving this burden so late in life fell like a dark curtain across the whole family. Although Jen lived with them and was always at home when she wasn't working, Leah maintained her silence and had not spoken to her daughter beyond what was absolutely necessary in nearly seven years. Worse still, her interactions with Harriet were saturated with irritability and impatience.

But if Leah let Harriet know that she was a burden, it was her much older sister, Jen, who Harriet feared most. It was Jen who fussed about her manners. It was Jen who soaped her mouth for sassy talk and sent her to the basement for failing to do her chores. If Harriet complained to her father about Jen's exercise of dominion over her, Fishel would always point out that Jen was much older and cared about how she was raised. Frustrated and without understanding the impact of her words, Harriet would reply angrily, "But she's not my mother!" That often ended in a soapy mouth for Harriet, who seemed to have only her father for an ally and even he retreated when it involved Jen.

Nevertheless, Harriet delighted in the big house and her large, if much older, group of siblings, especially the brothers who lived away from home and, in some cases, were already married to ladies with very short hair and even shorter skirts. The "Flapper Era" had taken the country by storm and small towns like Youngstown embraced it enthusiastically. Harriet's joyous laughter filled the house when Joe or Sid took her into the parlor to teach her the Charleston.

She entered Mahoning Valley Elementary School. A picture of her in first grade shows the beaming face of a tall young girl with straight-cut bangs who seems too old and too big for her class. Years later, when she was required to provide a birth certificate in order to get a passport, she was told that the school had burned down, destroying all records, including her certificate of birth. But by then she had learned to not press further. By then, she had a husband, children, and if she was still haunted by fears and yearnings she could not identify, she emerged into the world each morning with her characteristically huge smile.

That would all change in 1976, when Harriet was sixty years old.

September 16, 1976
Cleveland, Ohio
Harriet

"Hey lady, hey, you can't park there. Can't you see the sign, for Chrissakes?" A squat pot-bellied black man dressed in a uniform without identification or badges. stepped around to the driver's side. Harriet stepped out of the car. "I'll only be a minute," she said, holding up her small camera. "I just want a picture."

"Of this place? What are you, some kind of inspector?"

"I'm sorry," she pleaded, "but it's really important to me, especially today. I promise I won't be long." She raised the camera to get a picture of as much of the aged, depressing brick building as she could in one shot. Before the guard could say anything more, she moved to the sidewalk and part way up the cracked concrete steps.

She had warily approached the building on Euclid Avenue that once housed the Jewish Center, the hub of communal life for the ever-growing population of Eastern European Jews in Cleveland. The building was now a Baptist Church, a reminder that the inner city was once home to a thriving, diverse Jewish population that had since scattered among the suburbs outside the city.

The guard was now glaring at her, hands on his beefy hips. "Look, lady, I don't wanna give you no grief, but I got a job. Now move that car or I call the cops. Okay?"

Ignoring the guard, she quickly climbed the remaining steps toward the impressive double doors. She closed her eyes and tried to bring into focus the memory of the night in 1934 when chance had smiled on her.

The summer before Harriet's sixth grade year the family had moved back to Cleveland from Youngstown. She was told that her mother was desperately unhappy about being at such a distance from her family. Harriet was by then close to junior high school age and if people made fun occasionally of how much older her parents and siblings were than she, the discomfort was short-lived. She didn't mind being back in Cleveland, but she was confused when some of her cousins referred to her as "adopted." Her father assured her that this was pure jealousy on their part because Harriet looked like a movie star with her blonde hair, perfect nose and deep blue eyes. "Just like a real *shiksa*," several of her aunts would say.

Her older sister Jen still lived at home and still dominated her. Her mother, Leah, never interfered with Jen or took Harriet's part in the daily arguments about schoolwork, socializing, or going outside without a hat. Harriet's only recourse was to find her father and beg him to see her side of the dispute. It usually worked and it was obvious to anyone who knew the family that Fishel adored the girl he told people was his youngest daughter.

Abruptly, in the middle of ninth grade, Harriet was yanked out of the public junior high school she was then attending and was enrolled at Notre Dame School for Girls, a Catholic school not far from her home. She was distraught and no one, not even her father, would explain this bizarre decision. Nothing about this uprooting from her friends and school made sense, She was a popular student, especially with boys, but she was not a behavior problem and she was an average, if undistinguished, student.

Although no one in the family had made any effort to impart Jewish education to her she attributed their indifference to the fact that most of her siblings were married and out of the house. Besides, she told herself, women could not participate in the services and had to sit separate from the men. Obviously, the Jewish education of a girl was of little of no significance. But this move to a church school?

In the midst of the turmoil and her copious tears, she lay awake in the third floor room that had once housed Jen and Rose and heard her father shouting bits and pieces of whatever the argument was about. "A Catholic school taught by nuns? Have you lost your minds? Her father's usually calm voice was vibrating with anger, "What do you mean, 'just like her mother'? She's a child, for God's sake!"

Harriet went down the back staircase the next morning ready for her new school. The blue uniform supplied to her had the school name embroidered near the shoulder and a small cross appeared just below. She actually liked the uniform, the cheerful color of the apron and crisp white shirt and knee socks. She passed her sister Jen in the hallway to the kitchen and looked up at her hoping for some last minute reprieve. Instead, Jen simply grabbed her cheeks and squeezed hard.

"Be grateful you have a home and a name, young lady." Only Pa had offered any comfort, promising to walk her to school every day, although he would not set foot in the church building. Day after day, Fishel Leavitt took her halfway up the walk to the church school and he was there waiting when one of the nuns returned her to him in the afternoon. He always tipped his hat to the nuns and they always nodded to him in acknowledgement. No one in her household ever asked Harriet a single thing about what went on inside of Notre Dame.

It was shortly after her graduation in June of 1934 that she was scheduled to perform in a dance recital at the Jewish Community Center. As she now stood at the building's doors, forty some years later, she was amused as she recalled that in 1934, young ladies who were "at that time of the month" could not go on stage for fear that an embarrassing accident might occur. And so it happened that she was seated in the front row and found herself next to a good-looking, very charming and witty young man. He barely spoke to his date who was seated on the other side of him. For Manny Rocker and Harriet Leavitt, it was love at first sight.

They were married two years later in a small ceremony at a local hotel. Although no one said anything directly to her, Harriet suspected that it was the oddity of her "circumstances" that precluded a more lavish celebration. In fact, it was years later, long after her children were born and when she had largely forgotten the gossip that had plagued her during her youth, that she learned of a woman who had visited her prospective father-in-law just before the wedding date to chastise him for allowing his son to marry a bastard. "After all, Henry, you're a pillar of the Jewish community. This behavior taints us all." Henry, it was reported, threw the woman out of his office.

Harriet had cried when she heard the story, stunned by the cruelty and embarrassed for her husband and his family. But thinking back to that time, she remembered with affection that her husband had not been embarrassed. If anything, he had been filled with compassion and resolve. "I'm going to get to the truth of this matter if it takes the rest of my life." In fact, it would take most of his life and hers, as well.

October 30, 1948
Cleveland, Ohio
Jen

She was weeping quietly as she clinically observed the red ribbons of her blood gliding across the water, wondering how much longer she would remain conscious. Jen had not left a note for her husband, Jake. She thought about leaving a note for Harriet, but decided against it. What would be the point after all this time?

Jen adjusted her body in the small bathtub, turning her wrists with the oozing slices upward, as if in supplication. She wondered if she should, in fact, pray for forgiveness. She had never been an observant Jew and her husband, Jake, was uninterested in anything religious. The only altar he seemed to worship at was the bodies of other women. Thinking about this caused Jen to squeeze each wrist, wanting this over with before her sister Rose came by to visit.

Ever since Jake left Jen, Rose had been by her side almost constantly. Sweet but pathetic Rose, Jen's sister and her champion through so much of her life. When Jen met Jake in 1922, a widower from Pittsburgh with a child of his own, Rose had been thrilled for Jen. Within the first several years of their marriage, Jen gave birth to a son and daughter and the family had seemed to thrive. Everyone was relieved that Jen had found a man, a good looking and very charming man, and that Jen had thereafter seemed less caustic and angry.

It didn't last long. Jen found herself raising another woman's child, just as her mother had been forced to raise Harriet. As the children grew, so did Jen's irritability and unhappiness. Although she and Jake managed to hold things together until after the children were gone from their home, their departure made it a truly empty house. Jake was rarely there and after he began to disappear from home for days at a time, Jen decided to follow him. She quickly discovered the apartment he shared with another woman on Cleveland's West Side. "You bastard!" she had screamed at him when he'd arrived "home" from his other family, as she banged the iron skillet on the stovetop.

"Excuse me, Jen, but I don't think that a woman in your position should be throwing that word around." It was then that Jen understood for the first time that her husband had never been fooled about Harriet. And Jake held all the cards. If there was an ugly divorce with accusations of infidelity, how far would he go to discredit her, to hold up to ridicule her wedding night story that her torn hymen, like her terrible limp, was just one more injury she had tried to blame on her horseback riding.

So here she was and why the hell was this taking so long? She was beginning to feel drowsy and she did not want to miss the ending—her own ending.

When Rose dragged her, coughing and sputtering, out of the tub and onto the cold tile floor, Jen was furious. "You stupid woman. Always interfering where you're not wanted."

She never forgave Rose, but she kept that to herself. After all, Rose was the only one still living who knew the whole story.

September 16, 1976
Cleveland, Ohio
Harriet

Harriet maneuvered the light green car away from the Baptist Church parking lot and into traffic. She knew that Notre Dame High School was now abandoned, but the old building was nearby and visiting it was an excuse to put off for a little while her final destination of the afternoon. She was determined to remain in control of her emotions until this day was done.

She had promised Rose as much. "I'll just talk to her, Rose. I know Jen's dying, but you can't tell me that my sister is really my mother and expect me to do nothing about it. I've lived with the pain and confusion all my life. I at least deserve to hear it from her while she's alive."

She was still trying to sort through the fragments of the story that Rose had whispered into the phone in her raspy voice. "Jen got pregnant by someone and she would never tell us who he was or why she couldn't marry him. It was just before the war, so we figured it might have been a soldier—somebody not Jewish, I guess. You know Ma and Pa would never stand for that."

But this morning, with the phone cradled between her shoulder and chin, Harriet had felt little sympathy for any of her family members. "But why not tell me before this? Why torture me all these years?" Her voice was rising and she realized she was shouting into the phone, now tightly grasped in her hand. "Goddamn all of you! Why? Why?"

"Please, Harriet, please. This is killing me. I'm only telling you now because she's dying. It was a long time ago. There was nothing to do, so Pa sent her away. We pretended she got a job in Chicago and when she came home, nobody talked about it." Rose's voice rose and fell with her

47

sobs. "They put you in the orphanage and hoped you'd be adopted. Then Pa couldn't stand it anymore. We'd hear him talking to the rabbi about abandonment and sin, about Joseph and his brothers and about Ruth and Naomi."

Harriet was suddenly seized with the realization that nobody in her life was who or what he or she had seemed. Brothers were really uncles; parents were grandparents, and on and on. How had she not known? Why hadn't she pursued the rumors? She was aware of the stories and gossip about her. Illegitimate? Adopted? Definitely not Jewish! She had asked questions. She got no answers beyond looks that conveyed to her how deeply her probing hurt them all. "Don't you know that you are loved?" they would ask. "Don't you trust us?" They silenced her with guilt and looking back she felt embarrassed by her lack of confidence, by the absence of any sense that she had a right to know who she was and not just who loved her, but who brought her into the world.

Before their conversation ended, Harriet had peppered Rose with dozens of questions, still unanswered and equally important. "Am I Jewish? Who was my father? What year was I born?" She did not ask Rose what was for her the most difficult question of all: "How do I explain to my children that this woman they know as their aunt is really their grandmother?" But, Rose was done, exhausted. She would not reveal anything more and became increasingly agitated. Their conversation ended, as had so many others in the past, with Rose hanging up and then refusing to answer her phone for the rest of the day.

As she pulled the small, green Saab into the cracked and blistered cement parking lot of the abandoned church and school, Harriet relived her acquiescence to her abrupt removal from public school and enrollment at the Catholic institution. It was a punishment for something, but to this day she was unclear as to what her transgression had been. Of course, her exile to Notre Dame had only added to the rumors about her and to her sense of being an outsider—a misfit.

The beautiful stained-glass windows of the church stirred memories of mornings she spent at the far end of the hall, away from her Catholic classmates, evidently protected from an obligation to pray with the others. Her estrangement had been complete and she left Notre Dame High School with only one friend, a young woman named Jane, who moved away shortly after graduation and whom she never heard from again.

Yet it was the nuns, the Sisters, who had given her a unique and unanticipated kind of salvation. While her classmates studied their catechisms, Harriet was assigned one great book after another to read and digest. What began as a requirement soon became an enchantment. Most of the books available to her were stories written by Joseph Conrad or histories of the great saints, especially those of the Renaissance. Moved by the stories of martyrdom, she spoke glowingly in her daily English class about the obligation to heal the sick, free the oppressed and feed the poor. The Sisters who saw the joy of learning begin to transform Harriet's life nourished her love of literature. She read voraciously until the day she died.

When she had questioned Rose this morning, she had not thought to ask why she had been banished to this strange and foreboding place. Over the nearly forty-five years since her graduation, she had explored a wide array of explanations. She looked up at the church spire, still beautiful on this greatly diminished house of worship. She shuddered with the premonition that perhaps this mystery might never be solved.

After her conversation with Rose, Harriet had experienced a moment of sheer exultation. She knew the truth and that, at least, could not be taken from her. But the moment was fleeting and now, as she left the derelict edifice of Notre Dame, she was filled with dread, not joy.

At last, she pulled into the last space at the Margaret Wagner Home for the Aged. Leaning her head on the steering wheel, she silently prayed that she would not give voice to her anger at the woman who had never acknowledged her, who had listened to her bafflement and anguish and said nothing, the woman who had never claimed her— the woman who lay inside this building preferring to die with her secret intact than to make her daughter whole.

She stepped off the elevator and moved down the checkered linoleum hallway toward Jen's room. "Keep it simple," her husband told her from his office. "Don't jump all over Jen or confront her." She now wished she had accepted his offer to leave work and meet her here. In so many ways he deserved to be here. After each new rumor surfaced, each new perceived slight, the wound would re-open and stir up the raw confusion that lay just below the surface. It was her husband who, in desperation, had visited Rose many years ago, asking for the truth.

"You know the truth, Manny. You have a beautiful wife. That's the truth," Rose said to him.

Jen appeared to be asleep. The room was empty and soundless except for an old air conditioner that ground away at its work.

Harriet leaned down and said softly, "Jen, dear, it's Harriet. Please open your eyes, just for a minute." Jen's eyes opened instantly and sparked with recognition. Harriet breathed deeply and without looking away, said in an almost apologetic voice, "Rose called me this morning. She told me, Jen. She finally told me that you're my mother."

The way this scene had played out in her fantasies was always simple.

There was a look of shock on her mother's face, followed by a sigh and then a torrent of tears as mother and daughter embraced, at last.

But Jen's scream was piercing and surprising, coming from such a frail, old woman. "Help, help! Get this crazy woman out of here. Help me!" Jen was frantic, waving her arms about wildly, while Harriet stood frozen in place. A nurse's aide arrived and calmly pushed Jen's shoulders and head back down on the pillows. "She gets upset easily," the aide said in a kindly fashion. "Her other sister, Rose, was here yesterday and she did the same thing, if that's any comfort. Why don't you come back tomorrow?"

When Harriet told her husband the story that night, he commented sympathetically that a secret of more than sixty years becomes the truth if the secret is important enough. "You'll go back tomorrow and this time I'll go with you. It would be nice to know something, anything, about your father."

September 17, 1976
Cleveland, Ohio
Jen

The nighttime aide at the home was a remarkably punctual woman. Her children knew better than to show up late for dinner, and whoever had the shift after hers had been observed arriving with her outer clothing still on rather than keep the woman waiting when her day was done. So it was that the last check of patients on her floor always took place at exactly 6:45 a.m. When she entered the room, she sensed nothing out of the ordinary. It was only when she stood next to the bed that she realized the woman was not breathing. She had heard about the commotion involving this patient yesterday and she thought that it was too darned bad that these people weren't left alone to die in peace.

Jeannette Leavitt Kay was pronounced dead at 7 a.m.

January 6, 1986
Cleveland, Ohio
Linda

After Jen died, my mother began asking questions of other relatives, but they absolutely refused to speak about it. "Let Jen rest in peace," they implored. It was infuriating. My mother had never known a moment's peace and these people took no pity on her, only on Jen. Finally, one of Jen's other children found the birth record at Michael Reese Hospital in Chicago.

After that discovery, my parents went across the country trying without success to find Harriet's father.

I try to feel compassion for the woman who was my grandmother, but so far I have failed. I try to understand the nature of the times and the humiliation that would have accompanied the public disclosure of a child borne out of wedlock, but I cannot accept that the deception of my mother continued on a daily basis, watched not from afar, but up close and personal.

My mother, Harriet, died today and somewhere I have relatives who will not attend her funeral, people I do not know and will never meet. Without meaning to, we have all been part of a family's elaborate quilt of lies stitched together for their own protection.

-PHOTO ALBUM-

Jeanette in her late teens/early twenties (1906–1910)

Fishel Leavitt (middle row, 5th from the left,
with three of his sons at a celebration (1910 ?)

Harriet's birth certificate, a fair supposition given the evidence that Jen went to Chicago for the pregnancy and birth.

Harriet's 1st grade picture at McKinley School in Youngstown, Ohio.
She is the second person in the middle row.

Harriet, approximately 1936.

Jen's older sister, Rose, at about 75 years of age.

Jake Kay and Jeanette (1930's). He was a handsome man, a ladies man and left Jen when he found out about Harriet's true parentage.

Harriet, my older brother, me and "Aunt Jen."
My younger brother Andy had just been born. (1948)

Leah Leavitt, born in Poland in 1862, was Harriet's mother/grandmother.

Harriet and her father/grandfather born in Poland in 1963.

Harriet with her husband, Judge Manuel Rocker, at his retirement dinner in approximately 1982.

THE
BARGAIN

"**D**on't make such a big deal of it, honey," he says." Really, it's not that serious."

"I just don't understand, that's all," she says."I want it to be perfect with us, you know, just the way it used to be." She tugs at her plaid cotton knee-high socks and crosses her legs.

He says, "How about a little Tequila with soda? A little bit of the sour for my sweetheart." He looks at her, her brows knitted with worry, and reaches for her lower lip.

"See, you could pucker up for me, right sweetie?"

Outside a car door slams and someone shouts, "What's the matter with you people? Can't you park that fucking jalopy in the right place?"

She reaches behind her, elbow riding high in the air, and closes the window. Turning back, her nose captures the lingering smell of antiseptic where the nurse had lodged the intravenous needle in her arm. The wound is covered with a bandage, a small reminder for so large an undertaking. She turns to him and strokes his hand tentatively.

"I still don't get it. You were so hot for me. I mean, like, I couldn't walk across the room without feeling your eyes undress me. Don't you remember how I used to blush?"

"Baby, baby," he croons, pulling his hand back and tucking it under his thigh, "it's still like that for me. Trust me. Do you? Do you really trust me? Cause if you don't, well, maybe we're making a mistake here. I'm not saying we are, but trust is very important in a relationship."

She wants to snicker at that. She doesn't know about trusting him. He is the one who wanted to get rid of it. She didn't plead with him then. He said he'd pay. "It's a helluva lot less money than raising a kid, even a healthy, smart little bastard, what with the cost of everything these days. Believe me, baby, this is a bargain."

She picks at the pink bed of her thumbnail. "So, honey bear, did this ever happen to you before? Not with me, of course. I mean I've heard about this kind of thing, but don't they have something to make it hard? Jesus, you were so big that first time. When you got out of bed, I was sure you'd trip and pole vault yourself right outta the window—Jesus!

"You're a real romantic, ya know that?" he says," Listen, 'Miss Henny Penny The Sky Is Falling,' nothing is perfect. I don't want to throw cold water on your little girlie magazine fantasies, but nothing is perfect, not ever, call that absolutely never." He rolls away from her. She reaches for his back. He punches the pillow. She pulls her hand away.

"It's because of what happened, isn't it? I know you feel bad about how much I said it hurt, but that's all history now. Like the magazine said, 'One, two, three and its over', done, finished. Can't we just forget about it?"

The man sits up on the side of the bed. She notices that the moles on his back have little hairs on them. She feels a moment of disgust and quickly looks away.

"Let's change the subject, ok?" He scratches his lower back, his fingernails leaving long irregular stripes on his pale skin. "Do you want the Tequila or not? We're still good at that, right? Maybe a drink will do us good. Maybe two will be just the ticket."

"I thought alcohol made it worse. But, whatever. I just want you to love me like you used to. You used to call me your little kitten." She folds over her hands like paws and purses her lips. "Meow."

He looks over his shoulder at her. His eyes wander toward the ceiling and she follows his glance to see what he sees, but there is only the dirty light bulb and the painted ceiling with cracks running across it like an half empty jigsaw puzzle.

He is shaking his head vigorously. "Like I said, you gotta have a little trust, ok? I've heard about this from other guys. It's not like I'm that old or anything like that. It's just stress, just plain old stress. Hey, listen here. That whole operation thing was tough on me, too, y'know?"

She can hear the rush of wind in her ears, feel the pounding in her temples that makes her press her hands against them and hold her breath. She swings her legs off the bed, stands and walks to the small cardboard dresser against the door wall. She picks up a pair of tweezers.

"Here," she says climbing on the bed near him and raising herself on her knees, "turn around. I want to clean up your back. Then let's have the tequila. Like you said, maybe it'll do us both some good." They can hear the traffic from the street, even with the window closed. She goes to work, concentrating on the small hairs.

It's the least she can do.

THE
SETTING SUN

"**I** can tell you this much, Mr. Wade," the Judge leaned her large body forward on the massive elevated desk, "I'm in charge in this courtroom and I don't argue the legal niceties with defense lawyers. Now, where were we . . ."

The Honorable Nancy Kelley, recently appointed to the bench by the governor, an old friend who shared relatives from Belfast, Ireland, had already managed to terrorize the regulars in her courtroom including the public defenders, the probation officers and, occasionally, a prosecutor who dared to question her judgment on even the most the minor and insignificant of issues.

Flora Morikami had seen this woman with the dyed black hair arranged in bangs and a ponytail only once before during her incarceration at the county jail. At the pre-trial hearing several months earlier, the woman had not bothered to look at her, simply waved her hand to signal that she heard the plea of "not guilty" to the charges and walked off the bench.

But today Judge Kelly paused and looked around the courtroom to be certain that none of her words would go unnoticed by anyone present. "Let me be absolutely clear. There will be no second term abortions in my courtroom." Flora's sharp intake of breath made a whooshing sound in the silence that followed. She turned to her court-appointed attorney just in time to see the dark red blush moving from his rumpled shirt collar to his hairline. Tom Wade was prepared for anything from this judge with a reputation as a loose cannon. But, this?

"Um, excuse me Your Honor, but I don't understand what you mean." Tom replaced the worried frown that had crunched his forehead with a tentative smile as he gamely patted at the small dots of sweat that had formed just above his upper lip.

Judge Nancy Kelly raised her severely arched brows as her hands slapped the desk top of the Judge's elevated bench. The Probation Officer, a young woman just recently graduated from social work school, jumped up from her chair behind counsel's table, only to sit down immediately while looking around the courtroom and hoping no one had noticed her startled response.

"Well, counselor, here's exactly what I mean. I mean that this girl is going to spend some time—about four months I'd guess—as our guest at the Women's Prison. If she gives birth there, she'll have some first rate and, I might add, free medical care. If she gets out before the birth, she can go to her friends at the ACLU and see how much help they'll be when there's no way for them to kill this baby."

"But, but that not constitutional, Ma'am. With all due respect Judge, the sentencing guidelines specifically recommend . . ."

"You don't want to mess with me, counselor. Not on this one. We go to the same church, Tom, and I know from personal contact with you that you believe in the sanctity of life."

Tom felt a tug on his sleeve. He could feel his client's sense of panic as her chest heaved with the effort to control her breathing. They had only met once before today, but at the moment, he was more concerned with whether this judge would ever again appoint him to represent an indigent defendant. His livelihood depended on assignments like this one—no real work and decent pay if the judge liked you—and he had spent more than a few hours massaging his relationship with this unpleasant woman in order to guarantee a steady stream of business. His panic was almost as great as his client's, who had now stepped around the lectern.

"Your Honor, can I talk to you?"

Flora Morikami looked out of place. Her youth, her Asian appearance, and her height made her a noticeable figure in any setting. The standard issue orange jumpsuit hung loosely on her tall, thin body and gave no hint of the pregnancy. Her long and uneven bangs suggested the work of an amateur hairdresser—a fellow inmate, no doubt.

Wade jumped in. "I'm sorry, Judge, I told her that she couldn't talk during the sentencing." The lawyer was now mindlessly wiping his sweating palms on his suit pants, much to the prosecutor's amusement.

"Never mind, Mr. Wade. I'm not afraid to hear what this girl has to say. She's written me a dozen letters over the last several weeks, begging for the chance to get out and use her freedom to destroy God's miracle growing inside of her. In fact, I have them all here," the Judge waved the wrinkled sheets of loose-leaf papers above her head, "every self-serving, pathetic one of them. I just got one this morning, isn't that right Miss Morikami?

"Yes, Judge." Flora had no idea what she was supposed to say. This couldn't be happening. Even the prosecutor had agreed that she would be put on probation and it had to be today. She knew exactly the calendar of her pregnancy, she knew the minute, the second of conception. "I don't think I can have this baby, Judge. I need to see a doctor. I need to talk to my mother. But if I'm here any longer, if I don't get out right away, I can't get an abortion anyway. It will be too late. There would be real trouble for me, Judge." Tom Wade was saying something in her ear, but she couldn't hear him. Someone was screaming. "That's not right. That's not right."

The deputy sheriff, a massive black man known as Mac, moved quickly toward the defendant. "Shit!" he thought "I knew we should have kept her in cuffs." Flora's voice had risen to a pitch just a decibel point below hysteria. But it was the Judge who now concerned Mac most. Nancy Kelly was standing behind the bench, her face mottled with rage, her shouts drowning out Flora's cries. Tom and the Assistant Prosecutor had reached toward the defendant, who dropped to her knees in front of the lectern. Tom stood up in amazement, taking in the chaos and wondering whether the crap pay scale for appointments was really worth this kind of aggravation, after all. It was chickenfeed, even if there was no preparation expected of him.

It was quite a scene, but not completely unheard of in this particular courtroom. The judge was glaring at the gathering beneath her as the deputy sheriffs brought the defendant to her feet.

"Did I mention that it is my opinion that probation is not warranted in this case, no matter what the sentencing guidelines recommend?" Judge Nancy Kelly was breathing hard, still standing and now waving a note slipped to by her bailiff. "I have latitude. I have discretion. Forget what I said about anything else."

"Adjourned," hollered the Judge's bailiff.

"Sorry," muttered Tom to Flora.

"This way young lady," said Mac as he snapped the cuffs into place, jiggling them to be sure they didn't pinch the skin on this frail woman's wrists. He was glad this was over.

Flora woke with a start. She could hear loud voices in the hall outside her room at the Holiday Inn. She kicked off the covers and raised herself up from the bed. As she crossed the room barefoot, she wished she had left some socks on her feet to protect her from fleas and other dirt and insects on the rough carpet. Pulling aside the cheap white inner curtain she looked out at the lakeshore covered in a vast blanket of snow. She had never seen snow before, not even when she'd been jailed for months in this city as a teenager for shoplifting and credit card theft more than a decade and a half ago.

She glanced at the digital clock radio on the nightstand. It was not even midnight, but she knew that more sleep would be impossible. Her insomnia was not new to her, but unlike her father who had never accepted this nocturnal malady, she found that if she embraced the sense of aloneness, she would not panic as he so often did. Besides, it made no difference to her—it had not since they had buried the baby, Shirou, tucking him into the dark turned earth like a turnip.

The baby's death did not go well. It was no more peaceful or organized than his brief life had been. Born with Trisome 18, the small twisted body in which his spirit resided seemed determined to punish all of them for forcing him to stay in this world too long. Flora and his parents had believed back then that they were doing the right thing by pursuing newer treatments, volunteering for adventurous and risky protocols. Flora had no one but her immediate family to consult about this horrible, progressive disease that played out in pain and confusion on her baby's tear-stained face.

The doctors offered little hope. Worse, there were no friends, no other relatives, no one other than her mother to look to. She was now a permanent outlier in the Japanese community. The shame of bearing a child out of wedlock was not ameliorated by the tragedy of the baby's disease. If anything, saw the outcome as God's retribution.

As is usually the case with this genetic disease, first diagnosed by the Cuyahoga County Jail doctor early in Flora's pregnancy, a lifespan of one to three months is typical. Shirou was gone in 60 days, but he was never gone for Flora—not really.

Enough! Flora marched across the hotel room to the window where the snowflakes were drifting listlessly onto the shoreline below. *I need focus, discipline, energy,* she thought, forcing her mind away from anything but her purpose in returning to Cleveland, now in her mid-thirties and far more capable of doing what was necessary.

Flora reached into her small carry-on bag and removed the tea bags, the aroma escaping into the room and momentarily soothing her with its familiarity. She reached deeper in the bag and pulled out the wimple and black cape. It was important that it be free of wrinkles by tomorrow morning. She wanted to look her best, especially since Asian nuns were not a common sight in America.

Knowing that any attempt to slip back into sleep would be futile, she pulled the heavy, brown leather briefcase from the floor up onto the bed. The briefcase was quite large and it was shaped like an oversized doctor's bag. It was known as a "trial bag" in legal circles and that was its intended use here, at least in part. It might be necessary for some other functions critical to a hasty departure from the St. Ann's Home, but that really depended on the outcome of the "trial" and the possible penalties.

The winter sun rose listlessly over a frigid Lake Erie. It would warm this bleak landscape as the day progressed and, if things went as planned, it would provide cover for her departure when it set late in the afternoon.

Her cell at the Justice Center had looked out on this lake and she had stared out the small window for hours, wondering if the architects of this dismal, foul-smelling place had overlooked a design flaw, a mistake that would allow a desperate defendant to end her life. The only flaw she discovered had been created by her recklessness, her involvement with an addict who, in return for her adoration engineered her participation in a scheme to use fraudulent credit cards to purchase quantities of merchandise from big-box stores in far away states. The shame she felt after her arrest in a suburb of Cleveland was not only a consequence of her circumstances here, but because her parents in San Francisco, her loving, indulgent parents had no idea that she was living with a Chinese man or, far worse, that she had dropped out of school at Berkeley.

Flora took special care brushing and flossing her teeth, shaving her legs and washing her hair, even though it would be covered by a wimple, the head covering that was no longer part of most sisters' wardrobes, but was seen occasionally on nuns from other countries, especially those from Indonesia and Africa. In Flora's case, it was a crucial part of her disguise. The more camouflage the better.

It would be almost 2 o'clock in the afternoon when Flora arrived at the home and asked to see Judge Kelley. She had carefully calibrated the time she would have for the trial with the time schedule of the home—lunch at 11:30, afternoon snack at 3:30. With the time it would take to get to the airport for her flight back to California, it would be tight. She had to make a persuasive case for first degree murder, mount a credible defense and reach a verdict in such a short time that she felt a momentary panic wash over her.

She sucked air deep into her lungs and exhaled slowly, very slowly. "I cannot fail at this. I will not fail."

The cab driver knew exactly where the home was located. "My mother's aunt was there for a while, don't ya know. Not a bad place, but one visit was enough for me, I'll tell ya. You understand, sister, it's a little creepy being with these folks."

Flora leaned her head back against the cold faux leather seat. She watched the nearly frozen lake struggle to regain its claim to movement close to the shore. *Creepy*, she thought as the bile rose in her throat, *we find the disabled and the diseased creepy because they aren't what we expect of our species.* She had witnessed first-hand the discomfort of strangers when they were around her wounded, tortured baby. Their eyes would open wide, their lips part and their heads quickly turn away, unable to put words to their discomfort or to acknowledge the presence of the caregiver who must in some way be responsible for this awful outcome. And wasn't she? Hadn't she agreed to be part of this "criminal enterprise," as the prosecutor had described the credit card scam. But worse than that crime, hadn't she lain with a Chinese boy, the enemy of her family, the scourge of the Japanese community, and with utter disregard for the consequences of her treason, taken no precautions to avoid a pregnancy.

"So, sister, you a relative of the person at the home or just doin' your good deed for the day? You people amaze me, if ya know what I mean. You do all this good, but ya don't really get paid and the priests, they get top billing, don't ya know. It ain't right if ya ask me."

This man is very good at having conversations with himself, Flora thought, a habit she was familiar with since her Japanese grandfathers had done so, also, although in their case, the conversation was silent and the substance of it was only apparent by a turn of the head or a tug at a beard.

"Here we are, sister. 1:45 on the dot! Can I get that bag for you?

As the heavyset driver reached for the trial case, Flora snatched it from the seat. "I'll be fine," she said as pulled the heavy case out and set it on the ground. "Are you sure you'll be here at 3:30?

"C'mon now, Sister! Ain't I gotcha here right on time?" the driver had a wide grin revealing a missing lower tooth and blasted Flora with his stale breath. "Just joking, just joking." he said quickly, mistaking Flora's slight frown for annoyance with his tone, rather than the smell. "I swear, Ma'am, I'll be here, ya know, like on the dot."

Flora moved swiftly toward the front entrance which, to her delight, opened with sliding doors and revealed a large lobby with a number of men and women seated in easy chairs accompanied by an aide or perhaps a relative as they stared blankly at the large windows or the aquarium. The two black women seated behind the large wood and granite desk acted as though they had known Flora all their lives.

"Welcome, Sister. It's a pleasure to see you today."

Flora set down her trial case causing the large cross hanging from a chain around her neck to bang loudly on the wood facade of the desk. "Oh dear. I always forget that's in the way." As she straightened up, grabbing the cross to stabilize it, she set out on the countertop the card she had typed with the name "Judge Nancy Kelley—confession."

"Is she expecting you?"

"Oh, I think she should be," said Flora with a small, condescending smile, "Oh my, she definitely should be by now."

A map was slid across the counter with the room number and directions. "There you go, Sister. Have a wonderful day."

The door was heavy. *Probably for fire protection,* Flora thought, as she struggled to open it wide enough to allow for the trial case, her handbag and a coat. Once inside, she realized that the room was in almost complete darkness and the only sound was from the oxygen pump and a large overhead fan. The body in the bed was motionless, not surprising given the severity of the stroke that had put Judge Kelly in this dreary place.

Flora set about her business. First, the large white sheet that would become their movie screen was affixed to the wall beside the doorway. Now the tray table was wheeled into place at the foot of the bed. Her gaze was casting about for another table when she heard the rustle of sheets and turned around. The eyes of her enemy were fixed on her and Flora felt vulnerable and exposed. But those eyes saw a nun, not an accuser. Flora quickly finished her makeshift courtroom, moved to lock the door and turned to face the monster who had destroyed so many lives—but only one that really counted.

"Good afternoon, your honor, "she said, removing her starched white wimple and allowing her long, straight black hair to cascade down her back. "I wonder if you remember me. No? No recall of the young woman pleading for her release? Not even a memory of her screams, of the newspaper reporters crowded around your chambers, of your speeches at your church trumpeting your triumph over the baby killer?"

By now, Flora had moved slowly across the room and was next to the head of the bed. She dropped her head down next to Kelley's ear and whispered "I'm here to help you remember, Judge. In fact, I'm going to take your side in the trial that's about to begin here."

The body in the bed began to twitch.

"There, there, Judge. Nothing to fear here but the truth. Now since I'm the Prosecutor—oh yes, did I forget to mention that you're charged with murder?—I get to go first.

Flora went to the end of the bed, opened her trial book and began her argument.

Ladies and gentlemen of the jury, I am the prosecutor here and I will prove beyond a reasonable doubt that the defendant, Nancy Kelley, intentionally and with malice aforethought, did cause the vicious, brutal death of a child of two months by means of ordering her birth despite knowing that the child would suffer horribly and would die in agony.

Flora looked up at Judge Kelley and could see nothing but panic and fear in her eyes. She felt impatient and once again moved toward the head of the bed. "Listen up, Your Majesty! This is about you."

As I was saying, the defendant was the Judge, Jury, Higher Power and Grand Poobah of the proceeding that forced this baby into the world with callous, no, amend that, with hostile indifference to the pleas of her parent and caregiver."

Flora looked again at the paralyzed figure and could see a glimmer of comprehension. She jumped to the other end of the tray table and from the chair pulled on a high hat of black silk.

Flora bowed to Kelley and to the imaginary jury.

Your Honor, ladies and gentlemen, I am the appointed defense attorney for this God-fearing woman who believes in the sanctity of all life. Mind you, I haven't had time to actually listen to her story or spend any time with her, but like so many lawyers who she appointed to defend the indigent, I'll just have to make do.

Flora tipped her hat toward the Judge, and as defense attorney, resumed speaking:

Now then, as I was saying, my client was a fine judge in the best of Cleveland traditions. She took care of her friends, punished her enemies and infused her opinions with her religious zeal. It is outrageous that she should be charged. She should be celebrated for defending the unborn victim of a mother whose concern for herself above all else was going to result in the child's murder. If anyone wanted to commit a murder here, it was the mother, the prisoner, and certainly not the Judge.

Removing the top hat, Flora announced that they would take a recess to allow her to deal with technical issues. As she dragged the laptop out and set it up on the tray table, she stole glances at the patient and was stunned to see the deep hatred blazing from her eyes. Flora spun around toward the bed.

"Well, well, I see we've made contact here? Very good! This is the part I don't want you to miss, not one minute of it." She reached for the hand-held video control.

Court is back in session. As the Prosecutor in this case, I wish to present my evidence by high-tech means.

Flora winked at the patient in the bed.

What I am going to play for you ladies and gentlemen, is a recording of suffering so profound that I suggest you bring out tissues now rather than disturbing your neighbors with your weeping and running noses.

The video projected on the sheet and began without sound. It showed Flora pregnant and smiling for several frames and then it cut abruptly to a picture from an ultrasound. The word "Trisome" is scribbled in black marker across the film. The video fades to a picture of the new mother, Flora, holding a blanket-wrapped bundle against her chest. Quite suddenly the sound kicks in, muted at first, but the volume intensifies and we hear an eerie, disturbing, otherworldly cry of pain. As we watch, the swaddled baby begins to writhe and Flora, screams for help, holding the bundle at arms length away from her. A pair of hands reaches out to take the infant. We see part of the grandmother's face. She is singing a lullaby, but it is drowned out by the baby's screams.

Flora is startled by a loud, insistent knock on the door. She reaches for the remote, blankets the sound and calls out "Can I help you?"

"Sister, I've heard some reports about loud noises. Is everything alright?"

"It is, my dear, it is fine." Flora says through the locked door in her most soothing voice. "We're almost done here." The sound of thick-soled shoes moving away both reassures and frightens her. She's running out of time and there's so much left to do. She grabs the top hat and faces her bedridden audience.

Now see here, Mr. Prosecutor, this is a terrible thing, this baby suffering, but babies with these problems are born all the time and no one knows in advance or, if they do, ever dreams of killing them before they're born. Who are we to decide who lives and who dies. Only God can do that.

Nancy Kelley's eyes are smiling. She likes this argument. Flora, still wearing her defender's top hat, continues,

Now I'm sure the prosecutor is going to argue that the Judge is not God, so she has no right to decide what happens in this woman's body whether she has her tonsils out, a hysterectomy or a face lift. Flora's body, in its entirety, is like a boundary in real estate. From head to toe, she will contend, a woman's body is off limits. But we would argue that even if this is true, the state, or in this case a judge acting for the state, has the right to prohibit murder, even if it is inside the boundaries of the woman's body.

"Objection! Objection!" (Flora has flung her hat across the bed so it barely misses the Judge's head. Kelley flinches.)

I apologize ladies and gents, but the defense is making my case for me and that's not fair.

Flora raises her hands far above her head, her fingers in a V for victory salute. Turning to the top hat, now resting just below Nancy Kelley's chin, she continues:

So, sir, using your theory of state dominion over the individual's body due to the imperative to protect others from serious harm, we shall now proceed to do the following: Castrate all rapists, execute or cut off the hands of child abusers or wife beaters, cut out the tongues of those who blaspheme, remove the lungs of smokers who pollute and infect, sometimes kill, others and the list goes on and on. Too silly for words? Not at all, sir, for in many extreme religions and cultures, this violence is justified in the same way as you argue that Judge Kelley has the power to become a body snatcher.

Again the pounding on the door!

"Let us in Sister. We can hear loud voices and the cry of a baby. What is going on in there?" Pound, pound, rattle rattle, scream, scream. It is building to the ceiling, filling the room. The body in the bed is shaking and twitching and begins to rise. Flora adds her screams to those of the pain-filled shrieks of the infant in the video.

———————

"Mommy, Mommy, why are you crying Mommy? I want breakfast Mommy."

Her eyes snap open. She feels dazed until she sees the face of her six year old daughter, her beautiful, perfect child, bending over her with a deep frown of concern.

"Just a bad dream, Lolly."

Flora sits up in the bed and shakes her head to clear it of the hangover from the dream. The brilliant California sun is making its way into the room and Flora watches as it picks up the strands of red in her child's hair. This gift, this child, will never know about the other baby, the child who died in agony in the very room that Lolly now occupies. She will never know about Cleveland, Ohio, or the monster her mother met there in a courtroom. And she will never hear from Flora's lips that the monster prevailed and that Flora, the mother who Lolly believes can do anything, and will do anything, to protect her failed to keep that other baby safe from the monster.

THE
BRIDE'S DANCE

The oversized wheels made a loud crunching sound as the minivans rolled up the gravel road, headlights dimmed, windows painted over with psychedelic swirls of brilliant colors, colors now muted in the rapidly approaching darkness. The line of small vans slowed at a turnaround, cut their engines as if on cue, and waited.

Several minutes passed without any discernible movement. Only the sounds of crickets and tree frogs broke the silence of the night in Argentina. A long, sleek, black limousine announced itself with more diminutive sounds on the old curved road as it slid elegantly into a spot created by the vans. The workmanlike sound of the sliding doors on the vans and the "thwack" of the limo doors signaled to a thousand insects that a feast would soon be underway.

Nine men and one woman emerged from the vehicles. Only the capricious August moonlight, pulling a caboose of thin clouds, guided them through the grasses, some ankle high. They tread carefully: the tall, solidly sculpted figures of men with strangely shaped parcels pressed to their bosoms like newborns; the squat men with large heads toting smaller packages wrapped in cases of leather and, at last, the woman.

The men formed a circle in the nightlight. The woman, sleek in a black satin dress slit at the hem to show her fishnet festooned legs, followed behind slowly, teetering from side to side as she searched for the elusive firm steps of hardened soil. When she reached their circle at last, she parted her lips and all was still.

The first notes of the flute caught the blackbirds off-guard and they, always prepared for an argument, protested loudly. But the rhythm prevailed and the birds and the insects and the tree frogs settled in for the concert. The two men on bass and the man on the flute dove into the curve of the tango and, as the bandoneons crafted an entire orchestra from their buttons, even the pampas grass dipped and swayed.

The crows listened, the insects returned to their meals and the moonlight stopped by. The woman stepped into the center of the circle, her white skin brilliant in the darkness, her red shoes gaining ground with authority. An outstretched arm snatched her from behind, spun her around and tethered her body to his. She snaked her fishnets in and out and around his legs as they wheeled and swooned to the pulsing demands of the music.

She could see her reflection in the sheen of his black skin, an ebony so bold and deep that it seemed liquid. They danced, this black bishop and his white queen, to the exotic concert of love bequeathed to them by the gauchos whose sweat from the fields scented the bars and the brothels in the small villages far from the patrones of the city.

She had brought her trophy home, this daughter of privilege with the son of sombreros.

"Over my dead body," her father had said, as they stood before him in the palatial home that even tourists stopped to admire on their travels through Buenos Aires. She had heard, but not listened. Instead, she had leaned into the thin, dark-skinned man beside her who sang songs as they made love, turning each touch, each movement into an etude of enchantment.

"I'll see you in hell, first," her red-faced, thin-lipped father had shouted, standing spread-legged in front of the wall filled with portraits of their European ancestors: their pale, pinched, pocked, pinked and painted ancestors. Her mother had retreated to the massive leather wing chair from which she would later emerge to plump the sofa pillows, visibly relieved that "this" was over and "they" had gone.

And now, near the outskirts of the city, the music pulsed on. The dancers threw back their heads in pure ecstasy as they felt in every note the triumph of the tango, this choreographed embrace of their dual ancestries. Their steps were precise, the dance of the pampas perfected to blend the heat of the encounter with the danger of the design. A misstep meant disaster—a gashed thigh, a twisted ankle. They knew this, and yet they danced with abandon, their risky business on show for the world.

And when all of them were spent—the basses, the violas, the flute, the bandoneons and the dancers, they carefully picked their way around the gravestones of her ancestors.

Dawn had arrived, a new day sprang to life, and the bride's dance was done.

FATE IS
THE HUNTER

On the occasion of her fortieth birthday, Julia Morgenstern went shopping for a sperm donor. She wanted a child, she wanted to be a mother, and in the absence of a husband or partner, she chose the best option available. After many months of answering ridiculous questions from friends and colleagues about her obvious pregnancy, months of fielding unwanted advice and advancing a large chunk of her savings for strollers and car seats, Julia gave birth to a beautiful boy who she named Peter Henry.

"He needs a name with gravitas," she explained to her friends, "an important name that seems to reach across the years from earlier times."

The young Peter Henry had a marvelous childhood. Although Julia continued working part-time, financially buoyed by her adoring parents, she was meticulous about childcare, nutrition, education and, most of all, about safety. She canvased the smorgasbord of websites warning of toxic toys, swallowing hazards, childhood illnesses, rashes and radon, crib deaths and constipation, and every childhood illness imaginable. Her dining room table groaned under the weight of brochures explaining in graphic detail "what to watch for" and "when to call the doctor."

Julia's mother, Serena Morgenstern, would regale the ladies at her regular Friday afternoon canasta game with stories of the attention lavished on Peter Henry by everyone, but especially by Julia. "It's like watching a movie," the older Mrs. Morgenstern would say, passing the unsalted almonds to her opponents. "There isn't any aspect of Peter Henry's life that is not scripted down to the smallest detail. You'd think the child was made of glass."

An outside observer might consider Julia's obsession with Peter Henry's safety and well-being both oppressive and stunting. But for Peter Henry it was as natural as breathing and although he occasionally looked with envy at schoolmates who were permitted to ride their bikes beyond the end of the driveway, he was content to be told by Julia that she would know when he was ready for greater liberties.

It was the morning of Peter Henry's tenth birthday and while Julia stood at the porcelain sink washing and paring the deeply red and pocked strawberries to cover the angel food party cake, a loud crash from the upstairs shook the ceiling fixture that dangled over the worn wooden kitchen table.

"What's happened?" she shouted, running toward the stairs, the wounded strawberry in one hand, the paring knife in the other. Her short legs, that had recently abandoned any pretense of a willingness to carry around her aging, plump body without complaint, were suddenly game for this emergency.

Bounding up the uncarpeted stairs, she burst into Peter Henry's room and nearly fainted at the sight of her child's chin dripping with blood as he stared wide-eyed at the small metal make-up case lying on the floor next to the overturned wooden stool.

She had dreaded just such an event as this and had rehearsed over and over in her imagination what she would do first, who she would call and how quickly and confidently she would respond to the crisis. This was the moment of truth and here she stood, paralyzed in the bedroom doorway, fixated on the blood dropping like a leaky faucet from Peter Henry's split lip. *This can't be happening,* she thought. It was a parody of her recurrent nightmare, a dream that filled her with a sense of doom and never failed to leave her sobbing with guilt and remorse.

In it, she and Peter Henry were at a beach somewhere in Maine when the boy suddenly disappeared in the surf. As the dream tumbled through her subconscious in brilliant technicolor, she watched in horror as Peter Henry resurfaced and struggled to stay afloat in the crashing waves. But in this dreamscape she was no hero, she did not race into the surf without any thought for her own safety. Nor did she use her last bit of strength to reach out and grasp his tiny hand, snatching him from death's open door. Instead, she was rooted in the sand that had become like cement, her arms outstretched into the vast and endless void. No matter how hard she tried, no matter how loud her screams, no contact was made with the ocean and no sound was heard.

"This is every parent's nightmare," said Claudia, a specialist in panic disorder, highly recommended by Julia's mother who had insisted this was the proper diagnosis. The petite and soft spoken therapist continued, leaning forward in her Eames chair for emphasis. "The dream gains strength because Peter Henry is an only child. It would be well for you to realize that your choice of setting for this failure to protect Peter Henry is a perfect metaphor for the size of the task before you. Like the ocean, the gatekeeper's job for a parent is gargantuan. It is undoable. You cannot keep your child forever on the shore."

But this was not the shore, this was her home and Peter Henry's cry of "Mama, I'm sorry," broke the spell of the nightmare and as she swept up her little boy in her ample arms, the juice of the strawberry and the cut on Peter Henry's lip blended to form a burst of color, a field of poppies on Julia's starched white apron.

The little boy's tears were soon dried, the cut was carefully cleaned and Julia, despite her moment of paralysis, felt reassured that she could and would protect her son so long as she remained alert to danger. *It's my fault that he got hurt. He should not have been alone for all this time.*

Julia was a birthday enthusiast of grand proportions. It was a family tradition to treat each person's nativity day as though it had been decreed a national holiday. The elaborate plans for Peter Henry's celebration had been well worth the effort. It was late afternoon before all the cake was eaten, the presents opened and the games played. Julia and Peter Henry were exhausted and welcomed the suggestion from Julia's mother that the clean-up wait until the morning. "After all," chirped Serena, "there's always tomorrow."

As usual, Serena was right and tomorrow showed itself with dazzling sunshine that cartwheeled up the mountainside like a circus acrobat. Julia and Peter Henry finished breakfast and tackled the crumpled wrapping paper and ribbons with energy and determination, eager to finish their chores and head outside to enjoy the day.

Looking back, Julia would wonder why she hurried, why she didn't linger over her English Breakfast Tea, why she didn't pour her son another bowl of Cheerios dotted with banana slices. But the high sounds of the Colorado wind off the mountains whistled them out the door and up the steps toward the dirt paths that climbed to the foothills.

"You promised me. You said you'd let me do it, Mama." Peter Henry made a show of kicking at the small pebbles embedded in the dry, dusty dirt. "It's not fair."

"Let's not ruin our walk, Peter Henry. I'll talk to your Uncle Tom again this afternoon. I think it's too late for a little boy to stay up, in fact, it's way too late." Peter Henry knew enough about his mother to judge that he had already won a major concession. *Oh, thank you, Uncle Tom, thank you for coming to Colorado for my birthday.*

Julia was having similar thoughts as they began their walk up the sloping path. Her brother had called only a few days ago, typical of his impulsive nature, to announce that he was going to "drop by" for Peter Henry's birthday. Although she and Peter Henry had visited Tom on the east coast a number of times, her relationship with her brother was awkward and strained. She had long ago given up her search for what might have caused the distance beyond their obvious differences in temperament and lifestyle. Where Julia was cautious, Tom was reckless; where she was precise, he was expansive; where she was anxious, he was optimistic.

Her reluctant conclusion that all the foregoing might be merely gender driven was underscored when Tom called to tell her (not ask her) that he was on his way to Denver to see his nephew. "We'll do some guy things." That was all Julia needed to hear. She thought often and hard about the absence of a man in her son's life and, although her brother's home in Wells, Maine was almost a continent away, having him around for a few days was better than nothing.

When Tom arrived for dinner that evening, Julia was certain that he would agree to abandon the crazy plan he had proposed as his birthday gift for Peter Henry. But Tom was adamant and Peter Henry was vibrating with excitement at the thought of this adventure with his uncle.

It was after eight o'clock when Tom and Peter Henry left the house and Julia felt jumpy and unsettled by the unfamiliar emptiness. She thought about calling her mother to ask for some comforting words, but she knew that Serena would scold her for being "overprotective."

She finally settled on a glass of sherry and an old movie to soothe her nerves. She loved the films from the forties, so unlike the wild and frightening images Tom and Peter Henry were going to see at midnight. *Now I'm really being silly! It's a comic book character—it's Batman for heaven's sake!*

When Tom had suggested taking Peter Henry to the midnight premier, it had seemed so absurd that Julia had laughed out loud. "That's not a guy thing, Tom. That's an invitation to meltdown for an overtired kid."

For the first time since his visit began, Tom had reacted with the temper she remembered so well from their childhood. "Well, you listen here, woman. You're gonna raise a first class sissy if you ain't careful. If this boy's gonna live and have some fun, you gotta go for it. Ain't that so, Pete?"

Julia had cringed at the sound of the nickname for Peter Henry. But she knew Tom was right. What could possibly happen in a movie theatre in the middle of Colorado?

She awoke with the noise of her own scream. It was the dream again—her helplessness, her guilt—crushed her, as it always did.

"Have fun," she had called out merrily, waving vigorously as Tom pulled out of the driveway with Peter Henry safely tucked and belted in the back seat of the car. "Have fun," she had whispered again as she closed the door.

After the funerals for the victims, after the killer was behind bars, Julia drove to the cemetery where her brother and her son were buried. The gravestone for Tom Morgenstern was simple and traditional.

The stone for her son was also simple. It consisted of one word:

PETE

GHOST STORIES

October, 1944
Rothenburg
Bavaria

She spoke haltingly at first, conscious as always of her accent, it's harsh pronunciations, it's absence of melody. "I haven't had sufficient reason before this to share the truth with anyone. I appreciate that you seem willing to listen, but I warn you that it may, no—actually it will, change your view of me and of history."

She drew into herself a volume of the crisp fall air.

"It was dusk when it began. I remember that clearly because the high windows on the second floor, the floor where my brother and I were sitting before an easel practicing our lessons for our tutor, a rather nasty fellow who had a bad habit of picking at the hairs inside his ears, and—where was I—oh, yes, the high windows were like a kaleidoscope of reds and gold, weaving and wobbling as the sun set. It was a September sun and so it seemed to hurry down, not linger as it might on a real summer night.

We both heard the shouting from below. Nicholas looked toward the tutor who was busily tugging away at his ear, and we took some comfort from the fact that he seemed unperturbed. But then Mother screamed and everything was different.

I ran ahead, my blue silk skirt pulling at my ankles as I took the staircase corner too quickly. I could hear my brother behind me, panting like an overworked colt on a hot day, and I thought of slowing and taking his hand in mine. The scene below us, what we saw as we reached the last landing, was a tableaux of horror. My father was on his knees, his dressing gown torn apart and his undergarments exposed. A thin line of blood trailed from just below his beard to the marble floor. Mother was collapsed in a heap of yellow silk, fallen at the last step, her dark red hair springing from the cap that was tilted absurdly on her head.

Some of the men were laughing at the scene I have described, but the snarling soon began. There was no place for my brother and I to hide now. We had missed our chance and as soon as we were noticed, a rough looking bearded man appeared beside us brandishing an almost comically large pistol. No one laughed.

"It was apparent to me that we were all quite doomed and I tried to prepare myself for the inevitable. So it was that when we were ordered to descend to the cellar of the Summer Palace, I shook out my skirts and made toward Mother to assist her. Nicholas was almost carried down the winding staircase and as we turned the corner, I lost my way. Or rather I should say that some strong arms took hold of me and literally stole my body away. I was breathless with fright and the shock of being torn from the bosom of my family at such a critical moment.

"The night air was chill and I was brought back to reality in an instant. If I was to die, it would be as a virgin. No revolutionary ragtag lout was going to steal my prize and then my life, as well. I began to beat at the head and shoulders of my attacker, but he seemed to not notice as he crashed through the woods and toward the river. He appeared to be completely indifferent to my suffering as I bounced and slipped, now reduced to whimpering from the cold and fear of my fate.

"With my eyes toward the ground, I had no thought as to where we might be headed. Nicholas and I were rarely permitted outside the house and even on the delicious visits to the gardens, we were bundled up as though it might snow any minute, such was my mother's terror of burns from the sun.

Now, quite suddenly, my captor stopped and I was dropped unceremoniously to the ground. It quite took my breath away, but that was minor compared to what I next beheld. The man who towered above me was no stranger and was, in fact, my father's valet, a man my brother and I knew only as Gregor and rarely saw outside my parents' suite of rooms.

"Gregor," I exclaimed, nearly weeping again, this time with relief. "Where are we? What have you done? "Much to my surprise, Gregor placed a hand over my face, covering my mouth and my eyes, as well. His Russian was coarse and I did not understand all that he said, but it was obvious to me that this normally gentle man was determined to rescue me from my fate and that of my family.

"I won't bore you with all the details of my escape and the long tortuous journey that brought me here. I am telling you this now because I, that is actually we—Gregor and I—must once again escape. Our life here in this medieval village has been serene, protected by its walls, hidden in its hills. But our idyll is about to end. Those who might recognize me, more likely me than Gregor, will soon be in our midst.

"You see, we cannot escape this time without your help. How strange the world is to me. To think that I would be asking a Jew, who is herself in hiding, for sanctuary. But ask I must. We can pay you to join the ship's log of passengers headed to Palestine. And I assure you that we will be better Jews than our parents were Coptics.

"Will you help, my dear friend? Am I asking too much of you, you who have lost so many? But I, too, have lost and in addition to my family, I have lost me. I have no identity, no past, no picture, no trinket to remind me, no heirloom samovar to warm my tea. That is because I am already dead, dead to everyone since that September night."

The rush of words stopped as abruptly as they had begun. The silence in the garden was finally broken by the convent's bells announcing midday Mass.

"I've gone too far, presumed too much." She waved away her listener's look of disagreement. "No, no, I have offended you, discounted the enormity of your tragedy in my desperation to avoid detection."

Her audience stood to face her. The woman was tall and attractive, but her semitic aspect immediately set her apart from most of the residents of this small village. The Church of St. Jakob, the resting place of the prized Altar of the Holy Blood, had provided sanctuary for so many escaping a certain death.

"I must leave now," she said quietly, "Gregor watches and worries endlessly and he is not a young man anymore." She turned to go and had barely stepped into the light splashing onto the stones of the church courtyard when she felt the warm touch of her friend's hand on her shoulder. It promised nothing.

"My story may be done," she said, turning her head slightly to rest her cheek on her friend's hand. "It may be no more than a tale of ghosts ready to depart."

CPSIA information can be obtained at www.ICGtesting.com
Printed in the USA
BVOW07s2207280713

327139BV00002B/12/P